Read All About
CATS

PERSIAN CATS

LYNN M. STONE

The Rourke Corporation, Inc.
Vero Beach, Florida 32964

PHOTO CREDITS
©Norvia Behling: cover; all other photos © Lynn M. Stone

ACKNOWLEDGEMENTS
The author thanks Sue and Jeff Grzyb (Dream Babies, Crown Point, IN) for
their assistance—and their cats—in the preparation of this book.

CREATIVE SERVICES:
East Coast Studios, Merritt Island, Florida

EDITORIAL SERVICES:
Janice L. Smith for Penworthy Learning Systems

Library of Congress Cataloging-in-Publication Data

Stone, Lynn M.
    Persian cats / by Lynn M. Stone.
        p. cm. — (Cats)
    Includes bibliographical references (p. 24) and index.
    Summary: Provides an introduction to the history, physical
characteristics, habits, and breeding of Persian cats.
        ISBN 0-86593-556-4
    1. Persian cat Juvenile literature. [1. Persian cat. 2. Cats.] I. Title.
II. Series: Stone, Lynn M.- Cats.
SF449.P4S76 1999
636.8'32—dc21
                                                                99-30628
                                                                CIP

TABLE OF CONTENTS

PERSIAN CATS

Of all **purebred** (PEUR BRED) cats, the Persian is the most popular worldwide. Even cat lovers who don't own Persians know one when they see one.

The long-haired Persian has a curiously short, broad nose. It seems to stop almost before it starts!

You can tell a Persian by it nose, but not by its color. Persians wear their long, thick coats in many colors. But the flattened face, long hair, and stocky body make the Persian easy to pick out.

All cats busily groom themselves each day. But the grooming job is too big for a Persian cat by itself. Persian owners need to comb their pets each day or the fur tangles and mats.

This cat's flattened face, button nose, and long fur help identify it as a Persian.

Today's Persian cats are generally couch potatoes, especially if they've never been outdoors. But the Persian hasn't always been known for its easygoing manner. Some of the early Persians may have been little terrors.

Modern Persians are relaxed, easygoing cats. A quilt makes a good day bed during a lull in play.

Cats enjoy morning naps by sunny windows. Cats may sleep 16 hours a day!

One British expert on cat breeds and cat shows, Harrison Weir, said his helper had been "frequently wounded" by Persians. Mr. Weir decided that Persian beauty was only skin deep. Persian behavior in cat shows, he said in 1889, was "almost savage."

CAT BREEDS

The Persian is one of some 80 different **breeds** (BREEDZ), or types, of cats. A kitten whose parents are both Persians is called a purebred Persian.

Most house cats are not purebreds. They have parents and other **ancestors** (AN SESS terz) of many different breeds.

All **domestic** (duh MESS tik), or house, cats began with wild cat ancestors. The first house cats some 4,000 years ago, were little more than partly tamed wild cats.

One of 80 breeds of cats, the Persian is the most popular purebred cat worldwide.

Over the years, people who wanted to raise cats picked the cats that they wanted to bear kittens. These cat **breeders** (BREED erz) picked the smallest or biggest, lightest or darkest, longest or shortest furred. They also picked for behavior. By carefully choosing cats they wanted to have kittens, breeders helped create special types, or breeds, of cats.

Certain Persian cats, for example, have been mated with certain Siamese cats. The result, after many years, is what some people consider another breed, the Himalayan. It has the long hair and flattened face of a Persian. It also has the typical Siamese markings—light-colored body fur with a darker face, tail, ears, and feet.

A breeder combs a Himalayan, sometimes called a Himalayan Persian. The Himalayan has dark points.

WHAT A PERSIAN CAT LOOKS LIKE

The Persian could almost be the old English sheepdog of the **feline** (FEE LIN), or cat, world. But Persians don't wear their long, silky hair over their eyes.

A Persian's eyes are easy to see. They're large and round, like green, or, more often, orange saucers.

This Persian shows the thick, long-furred coat, large, stocky body, and short, bushy tail of the breed.

A Persian male (right) shares its quilt with a Himalayan kitten.

Although its head is large, round, and wide, the Persian has small ears. It also has a short, stocky neck and large, round paws. Its tail is short and fluffy. The whole cat package of 8 to 15 pounds (3.5-7 kilograms) is quite princely!

Persians—and some other cat breeds—differ within their groups from country to country. Animal breeders don't always agree how the animals they raise should look. How flattened, for example, should a Persian's face be? How long should its hair be?

Some Persian breeders prefer their cats with noses not so flat or hair not so long.

Breeders also have to take care not to create health problems for their cats. The Persian's very short face, for instance, can lead to problems with its tear glands.

This Persian does not not have the extremely flattened nose of some Persians. Her look appeals more to European than American breeders.

14

THE HISTORY OF PERSIAN CATS

Modern Persian cats began with the long-haired cats of the Middle East. Long ago, a region of the Middle East that includes Iran was known as Persia.

Much of the Middle East was warm. Warm climates tend to produce short-haired, slender cats. It is likely, then, that the long-haired cats of the Middle East developed in cold mountain forests.

A few of the Persians' ancestors were brought from Persia to Italy in 1620. At about the same time, long-haired Turkish cats were brought to France. The modern Persian is related to both of these longhair groups.

In the past 100 years Persian breeders have introduced dozens of new shades of color. They have also changed the cat's build to make it less bulky.

17

In the late 1800s Harrison Weir listed what he thought a Persian should look like. British cat breeders mated cats that would match Mr. Weir's description. The modern Persian breed was born—in England.

The modern Persian's fur is so long that daily grooming is a must. Some breeders keep their cats' fur clipped when they are not showing them. (This cat is fully furred.)

A Persian kitten practices what big cats often do—nap.

Animal breeders' groups don't always recognize new types as being true breeds. But by 1900, the many different cat lovers' groups had accepted the Persian.

OWNING A PERSIAN

The Persian, or longhair, as it's called in England, wins many hearts with its "baby face." Owning a Persian can be like having a baby. The cat won't cry (Persians are quiet), but a Persian needs daily care. Without it, every day is a bad hair day.

Many Persian owners avoid some of the fur problems by clipping their cats' coats each spring. A short-haired Persian won't show well, but it gives its owner a break from the cat comb.

Scientists have found at least 23 types of sound made by domestic cats. Most of those sounds are used for communication between cats. Persian owners find their cats to be generally quiet.

GLOSSARY

ancestor (AN SESS ter) — those in the past from whom a person or animal has descended; direct relatives prior to one's grandparents

breed (BREED) — a particular group of domestic animals having several of the same characteristics; a kind of domestic animal within a group of many kinds, such as a *Bengal* cat or a *Persian* cat

breeder (BREED er) — one who raises animals, such as cats, and lets them reproduce

domestic (duh MESS tik) — a type of animal that has been tamed and raised by humans for hundreds of years

feline (FEE LIN) — any member of the cat family; a wild or domestic cat

purebred (PEUR BRED) — a domestic animal of a single (pure) breed

The Persian looks much different than most domestic cats, but it shares a common ancestor—the small African wildcat.

INDEX

FURTHER READING

Find out more about Persian cats and cats in general with these helpful books and information sites:

• Clutton-Brock, Juliet. *Cat.* Knopf, 1997

• Editors of Owl Magazine. *The Kids' Cat Book.* Greey de Pencier, 1990

• Evans, Mark. *ASPCA Pet Care Guide for Kids/Kittens.* Dorling Kindersley, 1992

• Scott, Carey. *Kittens.* Dorling Kindersley, 1992

• Persian Quarterly Magazine, 4401 Zephyr St., Wheat Ridge, CO 80033

• Cat Fanciers' Association on line @ www.cfainc.org